P9-DVJ-752

BEING YOU

words by
ALEXS PATE

pictures by
SOUD

CAPSTONE EDITIONS
a capstone imprint

capstone®

www.mycapstone.com

Being You is published by Capstone Editions, a Capstone imprint
1710 Roe Crest Drive, North Mankato, Minnesota 56003
www.mycapstone.com

Library of Congress Cataloging-in-Publication Data
Names: Pate, Alexs D., 1950– author. | Soud, illustrator.
Title: Being you / by Alexs Pate ; [pictures by Soud].
Description: North Mankato, Minnesota : Capstone Editions, [2019] | Summary:
Illustrations and easy-to-read text celebrate things that make us special
and how we can communicate who we are to others.
Identifiers: LCCN 2018027869 (print) | LCCN 2018021415 (ebook) | ISBN
9781684460212 (hardcover) | ISBN 9781684460229 (eBook PDF)
Subjects: | CYAC: Individuality--Fiction. | Interpersonal relations--Fiction.
Classification: LCC PZ7.1.P3768 Bei 2018 (ebook) | LCC PZ7.1.P3768 (print) |
DDC [E]--dc23
LC record available at https://lccn.loc.gov/2018027869

Book design and art direction: Tim Palin Creative
Editor: Kellie M. Hultgren
Music direction: Elizabeth Draper
Music produced by Erik Koskinen, recorded at the Real Phonic Studios

Printed and bound in United States of America.
PA21

For my daughter Sxela, her friends, and children everywhere,
and the teachers and parents who are working to save them.

This story is about you and
the way your eyes will shower light
to open a path through the noisy night

You are a million years old
and tall as a mountain
fast as river water

a dancer
a singer
in charge of the game
the rule maker
Yeah, that's you

But in this world, there are whispers
that move through the air
like paper planes or falling leaves
They swirl around you

Sometimes they tell you
who you are
But only you and love decide

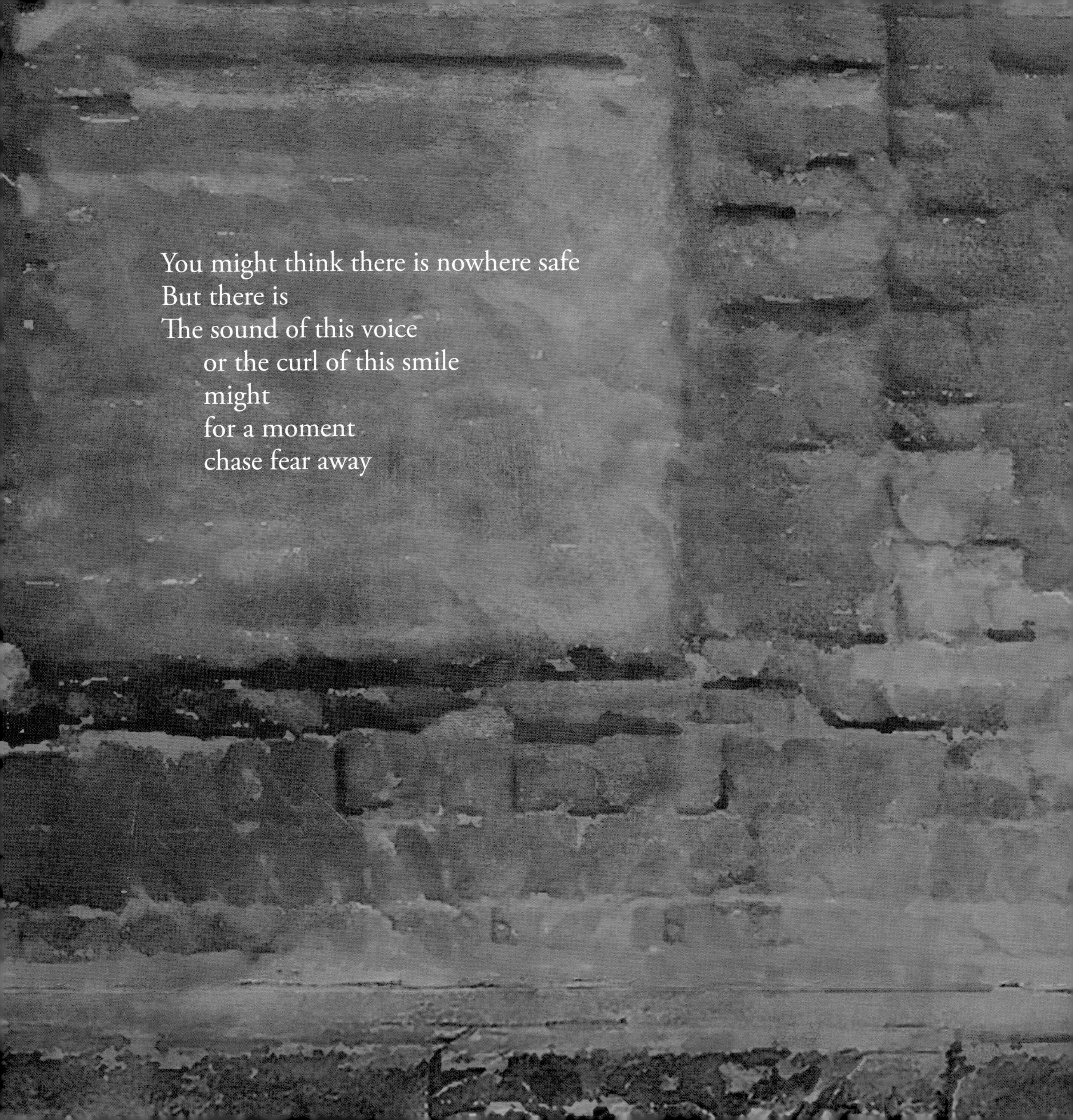

You might think there is nowhere safe
But there is
The sound of this voice
    or the curl of this smile
    might
    for a moment
    chase fear away

Watch a bird soar
and think,
Me too.

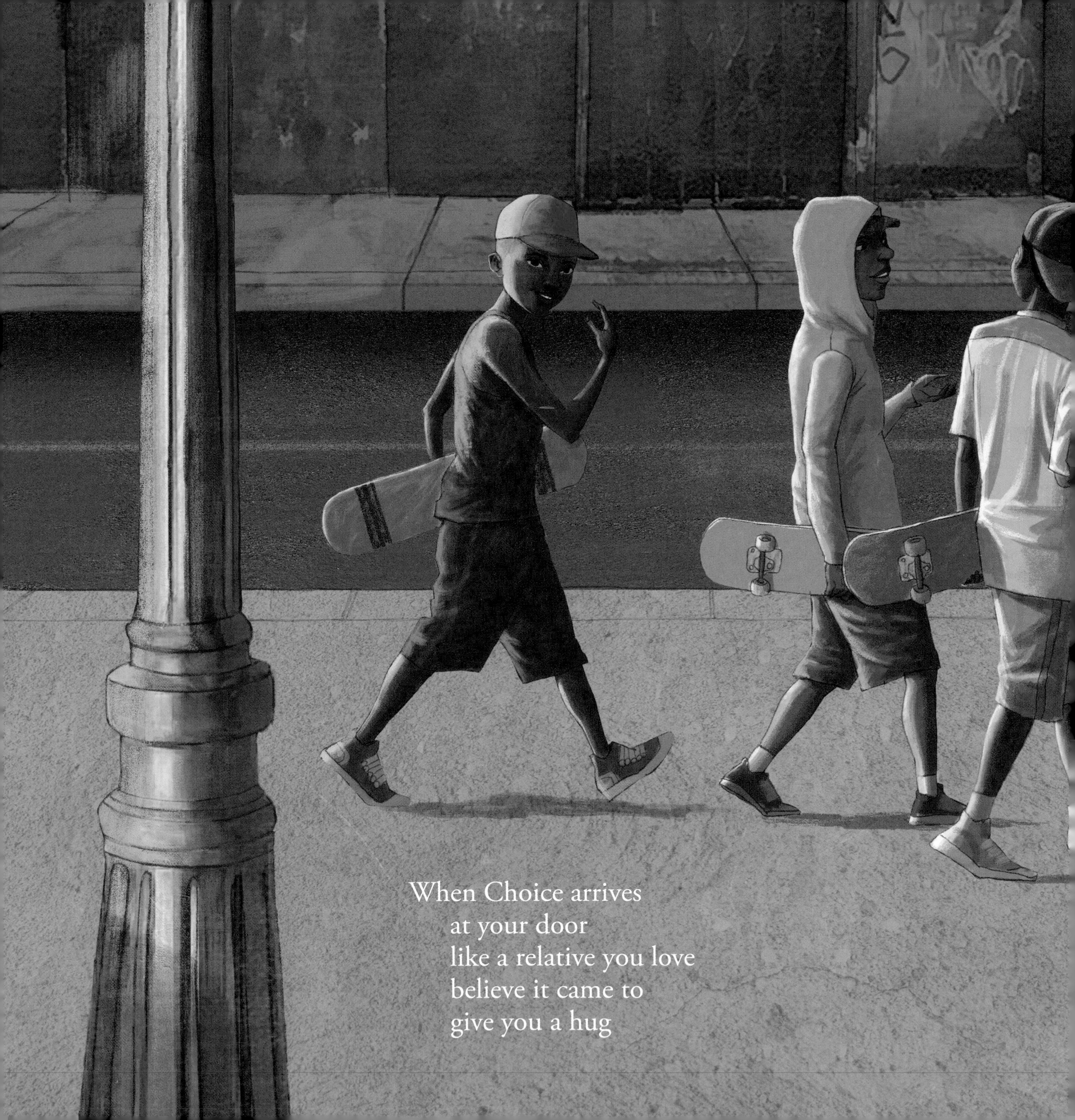

When Choice arrives
at your door
like a relative you love
believe it came to
give you a hug

FLYING

No body
    wants to be invisible

A body wants to be full and fluid
It wants to dance and slouch

It wants to see you nod and smile
    bcforc it collapscs on thc couch

If there was a sign on your chest
what would it say?

If it told your story
If it said who you were

FLYING

Would it say
    Here is the happiest
    bravest
    strongest
    most complicated child

        who wishes someone
        could read this sign

Would it say

I'm not who you think
I am?

I am strong
I AM CAPABLE
I AM TALENTED
I AM

It might say

If you look deeper
past my disguise
you might see me
past my shadowed eyes

They might say you are tough
Don’t take no stuff

But how far can you go on tough
before that’s it
nothing else?

Sometimes it's not the one
you expected
who can see you

sitting there wondering
when the sky will blue

ROOM

who sees through
    the noise
    and the trouble

Who can see
    you

It might just be a smile
that frightens the clouds
leaving you there

better
and still
you

Being You was written as a reminder that children should always be free to achieve their greatness. Their paths should be open, not blocked by negative images and generalizations about them. *Being You* is meant to soften the harshness of the way popular media projects images of children and provides a context for a new voice, your/our voice, as one that might help them navigate this reality. It is meant to continuously remind our children that this is happening to them and that there are ways to reject negative labels when they don't apply. Our first job is simple: free them to achieve.

Please go to innocentclassroom.com to see how.